Where Are You Hiding, God?

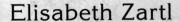

Elisabeth Zartl

Where Are You Hiding, God?

WJK WESTMINSTER
JOHN KNOX PRESS
LOUISVILLE · KENTUCKY

"Three, two, one . . . I'm coming!"
I take my hands from my eyes.
Where are you hiding, God?
I would like to find you.

I look for you in my room.

Are you hiding in the dresser
between my pants and socks?
I don't see you there.

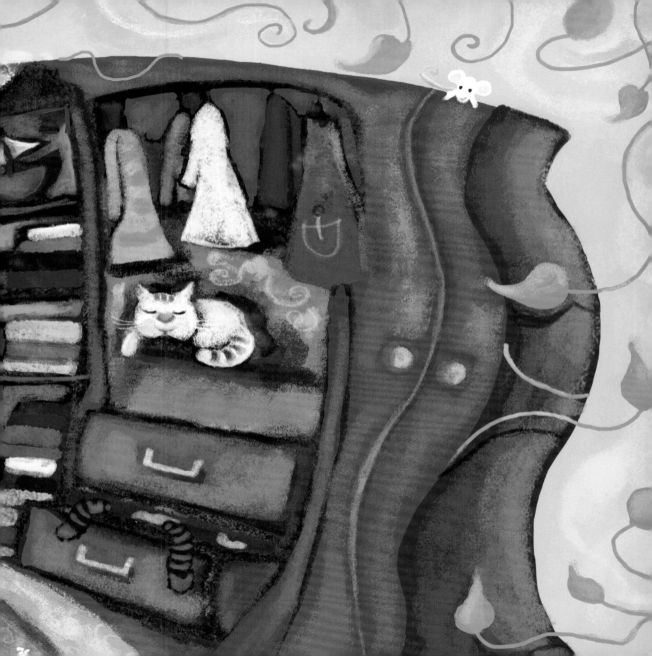

I look for you in the bathroom.

Are you hiding in the bathtub
under the washcloth
and my little rubber duck?

I don't see you there.

I look for you in the garden.
Are you hiding in the grass
next to the flowers and the dragonflies?

I don't see you there.

Why can't I find you, God?
I sit down under a tree,
wishing I could see God.
Then the wind blows a leaf
down onto me.

There you are!
I've found you!

You are in the leaf
touching me.

You are in the wind
that sent the leaf down onto me.

You are in the
flowers and in
the speedy
dragonflies.

I *can* find you
in the garden!

You are in the
smallest drops of water
that drip from the washcloth
and from the little rubber duck.

I *can* find you
in the bathroom!

"There you are! I've found you, God!"

You are in the **mirror**
on my dresser.

I *can* find you
in my room!

You are here,
and you are always
inside me.

© 2013 Tyrolia-Verlag, Innsbruck–Vienna

Original title: *Wo versteckst du dich, lieber Gott?*

This edition published 2017 in the United States of America by
Westminster John Knox Press, 100 Witherspoon Street, Louisville,
Kentucky 40202-1396. Online at www.wjkbooks.com.

17 18 19 20 21 22 23 24 25 26—10 9 8 7 6 5 4 3 2 1

Book design by Tyrolia-Verlag
Cover illustration by Elisabeth Zartl

Library of Congress Cataloging-in-Publication Data
Names: Zartl, Elisabeth, author, illustrator.
Title: Where are you hiding, God? / Elisabeth Zartl.
Other titles: Wo versteckst du dich, lieber Gott? English
Description: Louisville, KY : Westminster John Knox Press, 2017. | Originally
    published in Austria by Tyrolia-Verlag in 2013 under title: Wo versteckst
    du dich, lieber Gott? | Summary: After searching unsuccessfully for God in
    the house, bathroom, and garden, a young girl learns that she can find God
    all around her.
Identifiers: LCCN 2017023880 | ISBN 9780664263522 (printed case : alk. paper)
Subjects: | CYAC: God (Christianity)--Fiction.
Classification: LCC PZ7.1.Z38 Wh 2017 | DDC [E]--dc23
LC record available at https://lccn.loc.gov/2017023880

Printed in China

Most Westminster John Knox Press books are available at special quantity discounts
when purchased in bulk by corporations, organizations, and special-interest groups.
For more information, please e-mail SpecialSales@wjkbooks.com.